3 1994 01571 0640

SANTA ANA PUBLIC LIBRARY

D0387161

SANTA ANA PUBLIC LIBRARY

BEYOND EQUESTRIA

FLUTTERSHY
BALANCES THE SCALES

This book is a work of fiction. Names, characters, places, and incidents are the product of the author's imagination or are used fictitiously. Any resemblance to actual events, locales, or persons, living or dead, is coincidental.

HASBRO and its logo, MY LITTLE PONY and all related characters are trademarks of Hasbro and are used with permission. © 2018 Hasbro. All Rights Reserved.

Excerpt from *My Little Pony: The Movie: The Stormy Road to Canterlot* copyright © 2017 Hasbro. All Rights Reserved. MY LITTLE PONY: THE MOVIE © 2017 My Little Pony Productions, LLC.

Cover design by Ching N. Chan. Cover illustration by Tony Fleecs.

Hachette Book Group supports the right to free expression and the value of copyright. The purpose of copyright is to encourage writers and artists to produce the creative works that enrich our culture.

The scanning, uploading, and distribution of this book without permission is a theft of the author's intellectual property. If you would like permission to use material from the book (other than for review purposes), please contact permissions@hbgusa.com. Thank you for your support of the author's rights.

Little, Brown and Company
Hachette Book Group
1290 Avenue of the Americas, New York, NY 10104
Visit us at LBYR.com
mylittlepony.com

First Edition: July 2018

Little, Brown and Company is a division of Hachette Book Group, Inc. The Little, Brown name and logo are trademarks of Hachette Book Group, Inc.

The publisher is not responsible for websites (or their content) that are not owned by the publisher.

Library of Congress Control Number 2017954681

ISBNs: 978-0-316-47566-2 (paper over board),
978-0-316-47564-8 (ebook)

Printed in the United States of America

LSC-C

10 9 8 7 6 5 4 3 2 1

BEYOND EQUESTRIA

J FICTION CHESTERFIELD, S.
Chesterfield, Sadie
Fluttershy balances the
    scales

$9.99
CENTRAL   31994015710640

FLUTTERSHY BALANCES THE SCALES

By Sadie Chesterfield

Little, Brown and Company
New York • Boston

CHAPTER ONE

It was a perfect day in Canterlot. The sky was a crystal blue, and not a cloud was in sight. Fluttershy and her friends decided to have a picnic to celebrate Tempest's first month in Equestria. They'd spread a blanket out in the field beyond the castle, which had a view of the valley below. They could see for miles in every direction.

"Sorry I'm three and a half minutes late!" an exasperated Twilight Sparkle called out from across the garden. She was carrying a huge pink box, aided by the glowing magic from her horn. She set it down beside Rarity's purple tea set and collapsed onto the picnic blanket.

Fluttershy recognized the box immediately. "You stopped at Cinnamon Chai's shop?" The tea and cake shop was the best in all of Canterlot. Fluttershy had always loved their buttercream frosting rosettes and their cinnamon buns and their banana cream pudding. Who was she kidding? She loved every treat she'd ever had there.

"I had no choice!" Twilight Sparkle joked, and turned to show the dessert to the guest of honor. "It's not a proper Canterlot picnic party until we give you a taste of their famous chocolate-cherry cake. Just look at that rich chocolate frosting, that custard filling—it will change your life."

"Canterlot has already changed my life." Tempest laughed. She took a piece of the cake anyway.

"An alfresco feast with friends is so divine, is it not?" Rarity mused, admiring the dozen different teas with fancy names like raspberry hibiscus or huckleberry rose she'd brought to share. Rainbow Dash had brought ice cream and everything anypony could possibly want for a sundae—chocolate fudge, sprinkles, crushed candy bars, whipped cream, and cherries. True to form, Pinkie Pie had brought a selection of Sugarcube Corner's best cupcakes. It was all perfectly displayed on the dainty china plates and picnic set Fluttershy had found in her attic. She'd even folded the flowered napkins into perfect triangles as Rarity had taught her.

"What's your favorite part of Canterlot so

far?" Fluttershy asked before taking another sip of her Maretonian mint tea.

Tempest swallowed another bite of cake. "The ponies. Everypony is so kind. It's not really what I'm used to...."

"Oh no? The Storm King seemed like a big fuzzy teddy bear..." Twilight Sparkle joked.

"I definitely don't miss him," Tempest said. Her expression grew serious. "Or any of the Storm Creatures. Well...maybe Grubber."

"Grubber?" Rainbow Dash asked.

"Blue eyes? Always eating? He actually was a bit of a teddy bear. You probably never saw him, because he didn't like to fight," Tempest explained. She put a piece of cake onto a plate. "I'd always find him hiding on the ship, shaking in his quills."

"That's terrible," Fluttershy replied, feeling a

pang of sympathy for the creature. "I hope he's feeling better now."

"Without the Storm King ordering us around, I think we all are!" Tempest assured her. Even though it had been hard for Tempest to adjust at first, she seemed happier than she'd been in a long time. Those first few days in Canterlot, she was skeptical of everypony she met. When ponies were nice to her, she found herself wondering what they wanted and whether they were secretly out for something else. But slowly, with the help of Fluttershy and her friends, she was learning to trust. And even to have a little fun! During the group's visit to the capital, they were planning on taking her on a tour of all of Canterlot's best places: the opera house, Restaurant Row, and even the restricted section of Canterlot Royal Library.

Twilight Sparkle was especially excited about that stop.

"*So*...now that we're all here," Twilight said, plopping a big scoop of ice cream into a bowl, "I wanted to share an idea I had with all of you. It's about a school of—"

She was interrupted by a strange sound somewhere above them. The ponies looked up. A giant purple pelican swooped down around the castle, carrying something in its beak. As it came closer, the sound of its wings beating against the air grew louder. *Whoosh boom whoosh boom whoosh boom!*

"Well, *I'll* be..." Applejack stared up, holding her cowpony hat against her head so it didn't fly right off in the breeze. "It's a plum-pickin' purple pelican!"

"That is *quite* unusual. It's a long way from

the ocean...." Rarity marveled at the way the bird's plum-colored feathers faded into a pretty lavender ombré. She could feel the inspiration striking for a fabulous hat of the same hues. "What do you think it wants, Fluttershy?"

"I'm not sure, but I think we're about to find out," Fluttershy replied without taking her eyes off the beautiful bird as it flew down and landed just inches away from them. Now that it was closer, they could see it was carrying a white bag filled with seashells. It leaned forward and pulled out a glittering, pearlescent clamshell.

"For us?" Fluttershy asked, meekly stepping forward. The bird spread its wings and began a series of elaborate squawks. Fluttershy nodded along as she listened. "Oh, I see. Well, thank you very much.

"He says it's a special delivery from Seaques-tria Post! But, if you'll excuse him, he has a full bag today. . . . Lots of shells to deliver. . ." The ponies watched as he took off into the sky. "And he has to get going," Fluttershy finished, though there wasn't much point.

"Well, aren't ya gonna open it?" Rainbow Dash urged with an impatient hoof stomp. "Must be something super important if that dude flew all the way to Canterlot to deliver it to us!"

Fluttershy pried open the clamshell, and a rush of salty water came out. A tiny scroll was inside. It was tied up with a piece of seaweed.

"I bet I know who this is from," Fluttershy said as she unrolled the wet paper. The message was written in squid ink. She read it quietly to herself.

Hi, friends!

It's Skystar. Remember me? We defeated the Storm King together? Of course you do! I'm writing from underneath Mount Aris, and I guess... I wanted to know how you all were doing. And what you were doing. What are you doing up there?!?

Since we last saw one another, I've made six seashell picture frames, a seashell purse, and this really cool seashell necklace that holds smaller seashell necklaces inside each of the shells! I'm about to start a finstool made of abalone shells. I guess what I'm saying is... I'm bored! Are you bored, too? Would you want to come visit me down here?

There's no way my mom is going to let me come back to Canterlot any time soon, not after that stunt I pulled. And a Seapony can only make so many seashell necklaces, you know? And, really, how am I supposed to go back to my normal life when I just helped defeat the evil king who destroyed my city?!?

Anyway! Come visit... pretty please with seashells on top?

—Me

"Fluttershy!" Rarity said. She leaned forward, trying to see what the note said. "Come on, don't keep us in suspense!"

"It's from Skystar," Fluttershy said, laughing. "She's bored, and she wants us to come visit Mount Aris. She's stuck crafting seashell picture frames until Queen Novo decides she's not grounded."

"Being grounded to the ocean floor is just about as grounded as a pony can get!" Rainbow Dash commented, shaking her mane at the thought of it. Having grown up in Cloudsdale, she'd never been grounded in her life.

"*Oooooohh*, I'd love to go back to Mount Aris," Rarity said. "We didn't really get to explore because of the whole *imminent crisis* thing last time. Remember that cute street with all the tiny shops and cafés? I'd love to find some of that iridescent fabric that seems to be the current fashion in Seaquestria."

"That fountain was the most fun ever!" Pinkie Pie squealed. "It was like a twirly-whirly secret trapdoor to another world!"

"I hope you all have fun!" Tempest forced a tiny smile. She took another bite of chocolate-cherry cake to mask her discomfort.

"Yer not comin'?" Applejack asked, raising a brow.

"I don't think I'll be allowed back there..." Tempest said. Everypony else grew quiet, realizing she was right. Before Tempest was their friend, she'd been their enemy, working with the Storm King. Even though she'd helped the ponies in the end, the Hippogriffs and everypony in Seaquestria remembered her as the Unicorn with the broken horn who'd tricked them and stormed their city. Fluttershy knew Queen Novo wasn't one to forgive and forget.

"Tempest does have a point. I don't think Queen Novo would be happy to see me, either," Twilight Sparkle said. "Not after what happened with the pearl."

"She definitely wasn't thrilled about that." Fluttershy tried to find the right words. Twilight Sparkle had distracted Skystar and tried to steal her mother's pearl. It was a mistake, and while she was sorry, it wasn't the easiest thing to explain away. *Whoops! I lied to your daughter and tried to steal your most important possession! My mistake!*

"Don't worry, I'm sure there will be lots more chances to visit Skystar!" Pinkie Pie offered. "After all, we love visiting ponies all over the place! We're visiting you in Canterlot right now! Come on, we still have to take you on that tour. We're gonna see a show at the puppet theater or gallop through the hedge maze. Or play with puppets while we gallop through the hedge maze!" Pinkie leaned in and gave Tempest a wink. "It's kind of a best-friends tradition we have."

"It is?" Applejack whispered to Rarity, who just shrugged. It was better not to question Pinkie's random traditions and just go along for the ride. "Oh, uh, I mean, it sure is!"

"But what about your friend Skystar?" Tempest asked. "Aren't you the least bit concerned about all the…you know, *shells*?"

The rest of the ponies didn't want to make Tempest feel left out, especially when she'd been in Canterlot for only a few weeks. But Skystar was writing them because she was bored, and it did sound as if she could use a friend. How many crafts could one Seapony make? Wouldn't they be lonely underneath Mount Aris, too?

"I'll go see Skystar," Fluttershy volunteered. "A Seaquestrian sleepover could be fun. But promise not to show Tempest everything without me—I want to see her face when she visits the Canterlot Menagerie for the first time!"

"Deal." Twilight Sparkle smiled. They could always go back to Seaquestria together some other time. Right now it was better for the ponies to stay with Tempest and make sure everything went smoothly with her transition. Fluttershy would tell Skystar they missed her, and they'd see her soon.

"I should probably bring Skystar something, right?" Fluttershy asked, eyeing the remains of their picnic. It was always nice not to go empty-hoofed when a friend was hosting.

"If only this double-chunk chocolate ice cream didn't melt," Rainbow Dash said, popping another spoonful into her mouth. "Guess I have to eat the rest."

Fluttershy cut a slice of the chocolate-cherry cake and put it on a plate, then covered it with a napkin. "A little slice of Canterlot for her..."

"A bit unconventional for an underwater trip," Rarity observed. "But it really is the best cake on land, so I can't imagine it wouldn't be the best under the sea as well!"

Fluttershy packed up her stuff to go and took off back through the field. She didn't get far before Twilight Sparkle called after her.

"And, Fluttershy?" she asked. "Will you bring us back some seashell necklaces?"

CHAPTER TWO

It didn't take long for Fluttershy to realize the whole cake thing was a bad idea. It was hard to fly with a piece of cake on a plate covered with a napkin, and when she finally got to Mount Aris, there was no way she could bring it underwater without it getting soaked. What was she supposed to do? Present a soggy chocolate-cherry cake to Skystar and Queen Novo? Who would want to eat that?

Fluttershy put down the cake outside the gates and trotted through the ruined city. It was just as she remembered it. Pillars were toppled over. The buildings were broken and crumbling. Stones and bricks littered the street. She wove her way through the narrow alleys, going back to the castle they'd found all those weeks before. She had to climb over some rubble to get in.

The fountain looked exactly the same as it had the last time she'd been there. There was a beautiful lotus sculpture in the center, and the crystal-blue water swirled around it. She put on her bubble helmet, peered into the water, and took a deep breath. The first time she and her friends had gone under Mount Aris, it had been an accident. Pinkie Pie had been goofing around and was sucked under, and they'd all followed her down. But now Fluttershy would have to do it alone.

"H-h-h-here I go," she mumbled to herself, taking a huge breath. She took two quick steps forward and came to a screeching halt. It didn't exactly feel natural to jump headfirst into a swirling fountain. It took her three more deep breaths and four more pep talks before she could work up the courage to take the leap. "Okay, *now* here I go!" Finally, she jumped into the swirling water, letting it pull her below the surface.

Her bubble helmet, just like the one she'd worn the first time she'd come to the underwater world, allowed her to breathe and see everything clearly. It was a strange sensation, but Fluttershy was very grateful for it.

In the distance, Fluttershy could make out a cluster of bright, colorful lights. A beacon in the darkness. It was Seaquestria! She propelled herself forward, pushing her hooves through the water with ease until she came upon the familiar city gates.

The streets of Seaquestria bubbled with activity. Seaponies swam across the village square, gathered at cafés and restaurants, and floated along the aquatic avenues as they window-shopped at all the best boutiques. A spiky yellow crab stood in the center of the plaza, playing three instruments—a guitar, a banjo, and a tambourine. Six of his legs worked in time, creating the most beautiful music. Seaponies swayed in time to the beat, and a few had even started dancing.

As she took it all in, Fluttershy felt the excitement washing through her body, starting from the tips of her wings right down to the bottom of her hooves. No matter how long and how far she'd traveled, she couldn't help feeling happy to be back in this enchanting place. It was so refreshingly different from Equestria. And it wasn't just the beautiful sights—there seemed to be hundreds of new creatures to meet in the ocean! Fluttershy hadn't always loved the idea of being underwater, but now as she swam along, she decided to go with the flow, letting the water carry her in its current, moving her up and down.

The Seapony castle towered above the rest of the village. She paddled toward it, doing a quick spin as she passed the crab and the dancers. She couldn't wait to see Princess Skystar! They'd explore all the stores in the village and try all the best foods Seaquestria had to offer. Skystar had written her once about The Aria, a theater where singing starfish performed. Fluttershy had never met a singing starfish, but she was quite interested in asking one some questions. Maybe they'd go there and watch one of the shows, or go to the reef where Skystar had mentioned that all the rarest and most colorful fish liked to play. There was so much for Fluttershy to learn about ocean creatures.

Fluttershy felt herself clamming up as she approached the castle. Two huge guards stood on either side of the gate. Even though she'd met the Seaponies before, she was always a little taken aback by their appearance. They were magnificent and tall, with shimmering fins instead of front hooves. In place of tails, they had flippers, allowing them to swim easily in the water. The stoic guards carried coral spears and shell shields.

"Um, hello there…" Fluttershy practically whispered. They didn't return her greeting. They barely even blinked. Maybe they hadn't heard her through her bubble.

"I'm here to see Princess Skystar," Fluttershy announced, a little louder. "Will you please tell her that her friend Fluttershy is here?"

The larger guard was a deep teal, with huge eyes the color of blueberries. She leaned down and stared at Fluttershy. She noticed Fluttershy's hooves and frowned.

"What land do you come from, and who is your ruler?" the guard questioned. She turned to her partner and raised a suspicious brow. "How did you find our kingdom?"

"Oh…" Fluttershy felt her cheeks get hot. "I've been here before actually.…See, I'm from Equestria. Princess Celestia and Princess Luna are the rulers there. But I'm friends with Princess Skystar!"

The guard still just stared at her. The other guard, a shimmery white Seapony with giant green wings, circled her. "You're one of the same ponies from Equestria who tricked Princess Skystar," the teal Seapony said. "Who tried to steal the queen's pearl!"

Fluttershy tried to swallow, but her throat was tight. When they were last here, Twilight Sparkle had used Pinkie Pie to distract Skystar. As they were playing around the castle, Twilight Sparkle had tried to steal the queen's luminescent pearl. It was used to transform Hippogriffs and ponies into Seaponies.

"It was a bit of a misunderstanding..." Fluttershy said softly. "If you'll just let me—"

"I'm afraid we can't let you inside," the teal Seapony interrupted. "We're supposed to protect Queen Novo and the pearl."

"B–but I've been invited...." Fluttershy's stomach twisted in knots. Suddenly, she remembered the letter. She pulled it out and showed it to the guards. "Look! This is the letter Princess Skystar sent me. She wanted to see all of us. Maybe my friend did try to steal the queen's pearl, but she was also the one to defeat the Storm King. Your enemy. That counts for something, right?"

Fluttershy summoned her strength, remembering all the lessons her friends had taught her about sticking up for herself. She watched as the Seapony studied the letter, going so far as to flip it over as though it might be fake. She glanced sideways at the other guard, then turned around. "I guess it does. Apologies…You can never be too careful these days." She paused, staring at Fluttershy. "I'm Cerulean, and this is Salt Air." Then she pushed through the castle gates. "Follow us." She turned around and met Fluttershy's eyes. "No swimming off when we're not looking, okay?"

"Of course not!" Fluttershy smiled and let

out a deep breath, the bubbles floating up from her helmet.

She couldn't exactly blame the Seaponies for being so protective. Maybe the who-is-your-leader thing was extreme, but since Mount Aris was ruined by Tempest and the Storm King, they were notoriously on edge. They would have been suspicious of even Spike, who was just a baby Dragon.

Fluttershy swam close behind the guards as they entered through the gilded gates. Once inside, Fluttershy couldn't help letting out a tiny gasp. The Seapony castle was just as beautiful as she had remembered. There were glittering pillars and stained-glass windows. The great hall had a huge ceiling that you could swim to the top of. She was gazing up at it, lost in the sights, when she heard a familiar voice.

"Fluttershy!" Princess Skystar shot forward and threw her fins around her. "You came to visit! I can't believe you're really here! How long can you stay?! Oh, we're going to have so much fun! We can go to The Aria or see the octopuses dance in the village square, and, of course, we'll make seashell necklaces. Or seashell picture frames. Or bracelets. Oh, who knows?!"

"Can we also visit the reef?" Fluttershy giggled. "I'd love to meet some new fish!"

"Of course we can! I know *sooo* many cool fish!" Skystar floated up in the water, doing a few quick spins. Fluttershy couldn't help but smile. Skystar's enthusiasm was infectious. She spent most of her time alone in the castle, so nothing made her happier than getting visitors.

"Where's everyone else?" Skystar said, suddenly

noticing Fluttershy was the only one there. "Bringing in the luggage?"

"They wanted to come, but they're helping Tempest settle in, and we thought, well…" Fluttershy tried to find the right way to say it. "Maybe it would be better to wait awhile before Tempest returned to Mount Aris. They'll come next time. They all send their love."

"Oh, they'll have to!" Skystar replied. She looked only a little bit disappointed. "Tell them I miss them, will you?"

Before Fluttershy could answer, Princess Skystar swam off, waving for her to follow. She wove through the halls of the castle. "We need to get one thing straightened out right away," she said, glancing over her shoulder at Fluttershy. "Mom! *Moooooooom!*"

Skystar swam right into Queen Novo's

chambers, not even bothering to knock. Cerulean, the guard who'd greeted Fluttershy at the gates, floated opposite the queen. The two were deep in discussion and seemed tense. Neither took notice of Skystar and Fluttershy hovering in the doorway.

"This is all a misunderstanding." Queen Novo shook her head and sighed heavily. "I'd like to send another ambassador over to research the claims. The longer we wait to smooth things out, the worse the rumors in Seaquestria will become." Queen Novo procured a scroll and began to scribble a decree. "We don't need our citizens panicking in the streets."

"Your Majesty, I would be honored to represent our kingdom in the search," Cerulean offered with a deep bow. "If you'll allow it."

"Permission granted, Cerulean," Queen Novo

replied with a solemn nod. "But you must remember that I don't want—"

"Mooooooooom!" Skystar interrupted. "I know you're totally busy, but we just need the pearl real quick! Super-duper fast! For, like, two seconds, okay? Fluttershy's here, and she can't wear that silly helmet all night."

"Very well, Skystar," Queen Novo replied with a wave of her fin. "But be careful—and put it *right back* when you're finished, you hear?"

Skystar swam to the queen's nightstand and snatched the pearl off it. She brought it over to Fluttershy with a giddy smile on her face. "So you remember how it works, right? Just put your hoof there and—"

"Skystar!" Queen Novo barked. She was clearly on edge. "We have some very important matters at fin! So if you two don't mind, could you please catch up someplace else in the castle?" The queen turned back to Cerulean and the decree on her desk.

"Yeah, of course, Mom! We won't get in your way!" Skystar chirped, her big eyes staying glued to the surface of the glossy pearl. It glowed with a swirling, bright-white light. Skystar motioned to Fluttershy, and the two swam back out into the coral-encrusted corridor. "Ready?"

Fluttershy nodded and reached out to place her hoof on the pearl. Within seconds, she felt everything in her body tingle with a strange sensation. Luckily, she had been through this once before, so she wasn't afraid. Her tail and back legs formed one large flipper. Huge seawings sprouted out of her back. Now she was a Seapony just like everypony else!

Fluttershy swam through the water, faster

than she had before. It was easy when she moved her tail fin. She ducked and dipped and twirled, loving how it felt. It was a little like flying, only the water was holding her up. Skystar joined in on the fun, darting across the castle corridor and spinning around the room. The two friends giggled in delight.

"Not in the castle," Queen Novo yelled from the other room. "You know the rules, Skystar!"

"Come on!" Skystar called back to her friend. "Let's explore!" Then she shot out the door and down the hallway, racing toward the front gates.

"Coming!" Fluttershy called back, unable to hide her smile. This trip was already smooth sailing.

CHAPTER THREE

Seaweed ice cream with seaweed sauce and seaweed sprinkles on top!" Princess Skystar exclaimed, passing Fluttershy a cup full of green stuff. Fluttershy hesitated, then dug in her clamshell spoon and took a huge bite. It might've sounded weird, but it was delicious.

"*Yummmm...*" Fluttershy said. She glanced around at the other Seaponies enjoying their seaweed treats. "What's this place called?"

"The Seaweed Shoppe!" Skystar offered. She gestured to the massive menu. "They have seaweed sandwiches and seaweed pancakes, too, but the soft serve is my favorite! I'm so glad I get to share all this with you, Fluttershy!"

"Me too." Fluttershy nodded in return. It made her feel good that Skystar was having so much fun already. After their snack, the two friends swam through the village square. Everywhere she looked, Fluttershy was greeted with interesting sights and sounds. There was a craft fair selling sea-glass maracas and other fanciful items. Nearby, an area littered with food carts was being overrun by a small group of blue crablike creatures. They scrambled over one another to get to a cart selling fried seaweed tacos. Fluttershy gave Skystar a nudge and pointed to the critters. "What are those little guys?"

"Beezlebugs." Skystar scrunched up her muzzle in distaste. "They usually stay in the fields outside the kingdom, but for some reason we've been seeing more and more of them around...."

"Seems as if they came for the delicious food!" Fluttershy joked to lighten the mood. Clearly, Skystar saw the Beezlebugs as little pests. They were a little funny-looking, Fluttershy thought, but still cute in their own buggy way.

"Ooooh!" Skystar shouted, grabbing Fluttershy's foreleg and dragging her over to the center of the square. "This is my favorite!" A pair of octopuses were break-dancing by the fountain, their eight arms flying out in different directions. One grabbed a light pole and swung around three times, then suctioned onto the side of the Starfish Boutique. He let his

partner spin on his head awhile before jumping back in.

A small crowd of Seaponies had gathered around to watch, but they seemed distracted. They kept leaning into one another and talking, then turning away from the performance. Fluttershy didn't mean to eavesdrop, but she was floating right next to a pair of Seaponies who were speaking loudly to hear each other over the music.

"Do you think it's true?" a pink Seapony with bright-fuchsia wings asked. There was worry in her voice. "What Golden Fin saw last week?"

"Who knows? I always thought those nasty creatures didn't exist!" her friend replied, looking a bit frightened. "But what if—what if they actually do? We'd all be doomed!"

Fluttershy turned to Princess Skystar, wondering if she'd heard what they were saying. What were nasty creatures? Were they talking about Beezlebugs? But Skystar was dancing along to the music. She shimmied around, twirling and laughing. "Aren't these performers terrific?!" she trilled. "Sometimes my mom lets me come out here to watch. You know, as long as *I'm* being watched." Skystar gave a little sigh and rolled her eyes. "Such a pain in the tail fin, right?"

Skystar pointed to the two young guards who had been assigned to trail the princess and her guest everywhere they went. They weren't half as serious as the others, and sometimes when Fluttershy turned around, she caught them goofing around with each other. Fluttershy didn't remember so many guards from her last visit. Was this something new?

"Do you have to bring them?" Fluttershy asked. She glanced over her shoulder at the two Seaponies. Now they were tossing a conch shell back and forth.

"Yeah, it's a real drag, huh?" Skystar sighed. "But my mom has been really overprotective lately. Maybe if we swim quickly, we can ditch them!"

"Oh, I don't know..." Fluttershy frowned. "I wouldn't want to upset the queen again." After the last time, she felt she was navigating some murky waters regarding pony–Seapony relations.

"Don't worry." Skystar giggled. "I'm only kidding. We'll follow the rules...*this time*. Whoa! Look at that!" They turned their attention back to the show. The octopuses jumped and joined their arms, swinging each other around. Skystar clapped her fins together in delight and tossed a big pouch of sand dollars into their donation bucket. A few of the Seaponies in the crowd were staring at the princess. They'd obviously recognized her.

"Fantastic!" Skystar proclaimed once the dance had ended.

Fluttershy nodded in agreement. "Should we go to The Aria now?"

"Great idea! Actually, we're just in time for the matinee. If we hurry, we can even grab some seaweed popcorn at the concessions stand!" Skystar exclaimed.

"Oh! Yum, yum," said Fluttershy, feigning excitement. If she ate any more seaweed, she was going to turn green. Still, it would be worth all the seaweed in the ocean to see the buzzed-about show. "I've heard starfish have the most beautiful singing voices!"

"Just wait until you hear the harmonies," Skystar said, smiling. "Totally unreal!"

As they wove through the crowded amphitheater (with the two guards in tow), Fluttershy couldn't help feeling a bit self-conscious. It seemed as if everypony was still watching them. It could have been because she was with a princess. But Twilight Sparkle was a princess back in Equestria, so she was used to stares whenever they were together. This felt different, somehow. Was she imagining it?

She pushed it out of her mind and tried to enjoy the magnificent performances. Fluttershy had almost forgotten the strange feeling by the time a huge, curvy starfish took center stage for the final song. She wore a fluffy kelp boa and a long blue gown made of shimmering oyster shells. Her squid-ink eyeliner made her look glamorous, which reminded her of Rarity. Fluttershy would have to remember the style so she could report back to her.

"Feel the rhythm of the deep, down below, pick up your fins and do the ocean mambo, twist to the beat, fast and slow!" she belted out, bringing up two of her arms to clap out the rhythm. A light shone down on the stage, revealing three puffer fish backup singers.

"Do the ocean mambo, fast and slow..." the three fish sang. *"Ohhh ahhhh ohhhh..."* The fish in the center kept pushing the other two with her fins, obviously trying to get farther out front. She turned to the side, letting the light capture her best angle.

Princess Skystar and Fluttershy bobbed along to the beat. Skystar shrieked at the finale, when the three fish swam laps around the starfish, their scales glittering. When it was over, the two filed out of the theater, caught in the crowd of elated Seaponies. "There's nothing like a soulful starfish song," Skystar said, beaming.

"It was wonderful!" Fluttershy agreed. "The whole place was dancing! I loved the second-to-last song, too."

Skystar smiled, remembering the choir of starfish parading around onstage, singing different parts and clapping their arms together to the music. They'd worn incredible costumes of green and blue kelp boas with dangly shell earrings (of course Skystar had admired the earrings).

As they were swimming out, an older Seapony with neon-green fins came over to them. He wore a shell headpiece that looked rather regal. "Princess Skystar," he said, giving her a little bow. "It's so nice to see you here, outside the walls of the castle!"

"And you, Sir Aston," Skystar replied with a friendly smile. "Sir Aston, this is my good friend Fluttershy."

"What a pleasure," Sir Aston said with a smile. He turned back to Skystar, his brows furrowed together. "How is your dear mother doing? There were rumblings around town about a Seapony spotting a"—Sir Aston's eyes began to dart around in caution; he lowered his voice and finished his sentence—"a *Sand Dragon*. Is it true? Very troublesome, if so. I wonder what she's—"

"*Psht!* Don't believe everything you hear!" Skystar chirped, not skipping a beat. "But anyway, we've really got to swim. We're heading back to the castle now, actually."

"Please give Her Majesty my regards." Sir Aston bowed again. "I may be retired, but I'm always here to offer assistance, if need be." Sir Aston swam off.

"He used to be my mom's adviser," Skystar explained to Fluttershy. "I think he's bored or something. Whenever I see him, he's always trying to rustle up some gossip about top-secret Seaquestrian state business."

"So that explains what I heard in the village square!" Fluttershy nodded. "Some Seaponies were talking about Sand Dragons. But I guess it's just a rumor."

"Well…not exactly." Princess Skystar glanced

around, as if she was worried somepony might hear them. The guards were swimming at least ten tail fins back. "Down here in the water, there's a legend about great beasts called 'Sand Dragons.' Supposedly, they lived deep in the sands of the ocean floor hundreds of moons ago. If they are woken before it's time, they get very angry. Nopony has ever seen one....Until last week."

"What happened?" Fluttershy asked, eyes growing wide.

"One of the guards was exploring the surrounding areas of the kingdom when he found himself in a Beezlebug field. He heard a strange noise," Skystar explained. "When he went to investigate, he saw a giant creature with huge fangs coming right out of the sand! He was quite shaken when he reported back to the castle. He said the creature looked as if it could smash a whole building with just a flick of its tail!"

"That sounds scary," Fluttershy said. She'd dealt with her share of Dragons before, but the Sand Dragons sounded really intimidating. And mysterious.

"Don't worry! I'm sure my mom's got a plan," Skystar assured her friend. "There's always the chance that it wasn't even a Sand Dragon. Maybe it was just a trick of the light, you know? The ocean can be very dark outside our kingdom."

"*Mmmm hmmm,*" Fluttershy replied. She remembered that it had been pitch-black the first time she and her friends had found themselves below the surface. Skystar had rescued them by shining her light.

But now, Skystar just kept swimming, as if what she'd just told Fluttershy weren't a big deal. But everything was starting to make sense. The village felt different because it *was* different. Everypony was on edge. Somewhere, out lurking in the deep, there could be a big, angry Sand Dragon. Who wouldn't be afraid of an ancient giant, fanged beast?

Most of the trip home they were quiet, except for when Skystar stopped to point out a new café or her favorite place to collect shells. She even pointed out the reef that she was planning to take Fluttershy to tomorrow morning, before she left. They could look at all the colorful coral and glitterfish. Fluttershy followed behind her friend, but her thoughts kept drifting back to the Sand Dragon. Would Queen Novo really be able to fix everything? Or was Skystar being too optimistic?

CHAPTER FOUR

When they returned to the castle, new guards were stationed outside. They opened the gates for Princess Skystar without saying a word. The princess swam in circles around the great hall, her shopping bags under her foreleg. She'd picked out the prettiest blue shimmery scarf for her mother and brought back some seaweed cakes for all the cooks in the castle kitchens.

"Moooooooom!" she called out, swimming to the ceiling. "We're home! I brought you something really special that I know you're going to love!"

But nopony answered. "Maybe she's having dinner?" Fluttershy suggested as she swam after her friend. Skystar wove through the empty castle halls, toward Queen Novo's bedroom. But on the way there, she heard voices coming from the great gallery—a meeting place off the throne room. There was hardly ever an occasion to use it (other than game night), so it struck Skystar as odd. She motioned to Fluttershy to be quiet as they swam up to the doorway to spy.

The scene inside the great gallery was peculiar. Queen Novo and Salt Air sat in two of the huge carved coral chairs, below a series of giant murals depicting different scenes from Mount Aris. Queen Novo looked serious. The majority of the Seaquestrian guard force stood opposite.

"Cerulean has been gone much longer than expected. There is cause for concern!" Salt Air exclaimed, her voice twice as loud as it normally was. "And I will not sit here and wait to find out that she's been attacked by a Sand Dragon when we are fully capable of aiding her. Please, Majesty, let us go!"

"Enough!" Queen Novo barked, then spoke more calmly. "I don't understand why everypony is so worked up. There is *no* Sand Dragon! Golden Fin even admitted that what he saw could have been an illusion."

"Your Majesty." A smaller Seapony with pink wings swam forward and addressed

Queen Novo. "Please excuse my forwardness. I don't mean to swim out of line, but I don't think it was an illusion.... I think... Salt Air might be right."

"And who are you?" Queen Novo raised a suspicious brow.

"Coral Rose, the new Seaquestrian historian, at your service." The small Seapony bowed, eyes downcast. "I believe that the Sand Dragon is real, and it's awake." At this, Salt Air's face flashed a triumphant expression, only to morph back into one of extreme worry. Cerulean could really be in danger. Coral Rose shifted around nervously. "I... I can prove it."

"You can?" Queen Novo asked. She leaned forward in her chair. Her attention had clearly been piqued. "How?"

"It's all right here in the legend, Majesty,"

Coral Rose said, scrambling to unfurl a scroll. "We are due for what is called the 'Dragon's Morning.' Every hundred moons, supposedly the Sand Dragons awaken from their hibernation deep in the sand. They wake up quite hungry and go looking for—"

"For Seaponies?!" Skystar's voice echoed through the gallery. The guards froze, noticing Skystar and Fluttershy floating in the doorway. "It's true?!" the princess shouted, swimming inside the room. Fluttershy followed behind, feeling awkward and out of place. "Seaquestria really *could* be in danger?"

"Skystar! There you are." Queen Novo looked quite relieved to see her daughter. "Go to your chambers and visit with Fluttershy there, okay? The castle needs to be on lockdown until we know more."

"But Cerulean's out there...." Skystar's eyes went wide. "And I want to help! Are we going to rescue her?"

"Yes," Queen Novo said decidedly. She exchanged a look with Salt Air. "Tonight."

"Then I'll go get my things!" Skystar said, her voice trembling. "Wait for me!" Skystar shot out of the room, leaving only a trail of bubbles behind her.

A trail of bubbles...and Fluttershy. She moved behind a group of guards in a feeble attempt to hide. This was not how she'd pictured the evening unfolding.

"I know my daughter well enough to know that she is determined to go—no matter what I tell her to do." Queen Novo swam back and forth, then back and forth again, pacing the room. "Salt Air, you must watch out for her."

"Of course, Your Majesty." Salt Air brought her fin to her chest in salute.

Queen Novo nodded before adding, "And so must you, Fluttershy."

It was as if the water had drained from the room. Fluttershy suddenly felt all eyes on her. There had to be a mistake! Fluttershy was not even really a part of this kingdom. She was just a visitor. Why would they want her along on such an important Seapony mission?

"M-m-m-me?" she stuttered, meeting the queen's eyes. She looked worried, her brows drawn together in a line.

"Yes. Skystar has told me of your many brave pursuits in your land. And my daughter trusts you. Please, Fluttershy? We have already suffered through a great war with the Storm King in Mount Aris. We cannot take another tragedy."

Fluttershy didn't know what to say. But she knew one thing for sure—a friend needed her. And she never turned her back on a friend in need. "Okay, I'll go."

"We have to resolve this however we can," Queen Novo said, her voice full of sadness and worry. She'd worked so hard to keep the peace in Seaquestria. It was vital that it remain so. She put a fin on Fluttershy's shoulder. "Please be careful out there."

"Exactly! We must take precautions to protect ourselves from the monster!" Salt Air said to a Seapony standing in the back of the crowd. "Let's bring our coral spears and shell shields. Helmets, chest plates. Full armor. I'm not taking any chances."

Suddenly, Skystar reappeared. She wore a

saddlebag that had been decorated with shells. "What'd I miss?"

Fluttershy struggled to find the words to explain the quick turn of events. In a moment's time, talk had turned from keeping peace to wielding weapons. She knew she'd have a hard time persuading Salt Air to not go at all, but there had to be a better way. Wouldn't showing up in armor make everything worse? Bringing a small army with spears and shields? If Cerulean wasn't already in danger, she surely would be if the Sand Dragon thought the Seaponies wanted to harm it.

"Don't you think the spears will scare it?" Fluttershy asked. She'd encountered so many other scary creatures before. She'd tamed a cockatrice, a Manticore, and even befriended a Draconequus. There were fierce Dragons in Equestria, and she imagined a Sand Dragon must look a lot like that.

"I hope so," replied Salt Air with a huff.

Fluttershy frowned. "There's always another way to communicate. You just have to try to understand the other creature...." She looked to Coral Rose for backup, but the Seapony just shrugged. Up until recently, Sand Dragons had only been a legend, passed on to the Seaponies from the ancient fish and crustaceans. Now they were real.

Salt Air leaned in closer. "Giants of the Sea, is what the stories call them..." she said. "Huge fangs! Tiny, beady eyes."

"And claws that could cut you in two!" another guard added. The rest of the Seaponies nodded along, their eyes wide in fear. Fluttershy tried to keep her expression normal, but her stomach was doing flips. It was always a little scary to confront a creature ten times your size, and when Fluttershy had done it in the past, she'd felt the same nervousness. But she'd never let that stop her before, and she couldn't let it stop her now. Being brave wasn't about not feeling any fear. It was about not letting your fear stop you.

"Every minute that Cerulean is near it, she is in danger," Salt Air added. "We must give the monster a great show of force. It should know that Seaponies are not to be messed with!"

A Seapony who had left now returned carrying a bundle of spears. The end of each was carved into a razor-sharp point. Helmets were piled on the floor. There were chest plates and shields, along with a few other weapons Fluttershy didn't recognize.

"Moooom!" Skystar finally said. "We're not really going to bring all that junk, are we?"

Queen Novo looked as if she was struggling with the decision, too. Finally, she spoke: "You must stay safe. At all costs."

"It's not just the Sand Dragon we have to worry about," Salt Air said. "Cerulean is the only Seapony to have ventured that far beyond the village. We have no idea what we'll find out there...."

"It's all going to be okay," Fluttershy said. But as more Seaponies entered the meeting room with more shell shields and weapons, Fluttershy grew nervous. Part of keeping Seaquestria safe meant keeping the Sand Dragon calm. How would Fluttershy be able to do that when Salt Air was already so angry? What would the

Sand Dragon think when they showed up to its lair with a small army?

Fluttershy packed up a bag with food and supplies, trying to ignore the fear that was growing in her chest. But she had the sinking feeling that they were all swimming in the dark on this one.

CHAPTER FIVE

Is this the only map we have?" Fluttershy asked. She stared down at the scroll spread out on the table. It was a detailed map of the village, with every street and alley marked. There was The Aria and the square where she and Skystar had seen the octopuses perform. There were dozens of apartment buildings, two markets, and Seaquestria's School for Stalwart Seaponies. Almost every lamppost and street sign was marked. But beyond the village, the map was mostly blank. There were two kelp forests and a Beezlebug field that Fluttershy had heard about, but not much else.

"This is the best map we've got." Salt Air pointed to a blue *X* far out beyond the village. "This is where we think the Sand Dragon could be. Cerulean told us she was going to look beyond the kelp forest before she left."

"There's a tunnel somewhere close to this valley. We know that," said Coral Rose, pointing to an area far beyond the city. "In the legend, the Sand Dragons bury themselves deep below the sand. Perhaps the tunnel is an old Sand Dragon burrow? It could be a good place to start."

Fluttershy let out a deep breath. She knew it would be hard to negotiate with a mysterious mystical creature like a Sand Dragon, but she had no idea it would be just as hard to find it. They were leaving any minute, and they still had only a few clues about where they were headed.

"What about the Beezlebugs?" Fluttershy asked.

"Seaquestria is a young world," Salt Air explained. "The Sand Dragons have been underwater for centuries, but we only left Mount Aris two moons ago. We've managed to do so much in that time, but there's still so much we need to see and explore. We don't know much about the rest of this world."

"Nopony goes beyond the village, because we don't have to," Coral Rose explained. "But if Golden Fin and Cerulean can find the Sand Dragon's lair, then we can, too."

Just then they heard shouts and cries outside the castle. They bolted to the front windows, looking out at the castle gates below. A horde of Beezlebugs had overtaken the main square, darting into restaurants and every which way. Seaponies swam out of the way in disgust at the kingdom pests.

"What in Seaquestria are they all doing here?" Fluttershy asked.

"That's a really good question!" Skystar replied. She pointed to The Seaweed Shoppe in the distance, where a group of Beezlebugs had started gathering. "Maybe they came for the soft serve?"

Salt Air held up her coral spear. It was twice the size of the others, with a hooked tip decorated with fish teeth. "We don't have time to float around, talking about such petty matters!" she cried. "We have to go find Cerulean—now!"

It took only a few seconds for Salt Air to rally the rest of the guards. She grabbed a seaweed sack that was filled with food and supplies and threw it over her shoulder. Fluttershy wanted to tell her to be careful. If the Seaquestrians out in the square saw them all leaving in such a rush, carrying spears, they might be frightened. Widespread panic was the last thing they needed on top of a random Beezlebug infestation.

But Salt Air didn't look as if she wanted to be questioned. She swam past Fluttershy and Skystar, straight out of the room. "Line up!" she called out, and the Seaponies fell into line behind her. "Tonight we will defend our kingdom!"

The Seaponies all cheered. Then Salt Air led them through the great hall toward the main gate. As soon as the doors opened, the villagers began to gather and watch. Fluttershy could hear the whispers rushing through the crowd like a wave. Where were the guards going?

"Is it a Sand Dragon?!" one Seapony yelled as they passed.

"Are we in danger?" another called out.

Fluttershy followed along behind the army, more nervous than she'd been all day. More villagers were showing up by the minute. Some leaned out of their windows as the brigade passed, lifting up their Seafoals to watch the curious sight. Others lined the street. Through it all, Salt Air swam out in front of the guards, stone-faced and determined.

"Please swim aside!" she called, raising her spear in the air. "This is none of your concern!"

"Have a lovely day!" Skystar added, to make it all sound a bit friendlier.

As they got closer to the edge of the village, Fluttershy stared out at the water beyond the buildings. It grew dark and murky once the lampposts disappeared. It was impossible to know what was out there. She kept going, though, following behind the rest of the guards.

Fluttershy looked right, then looked left. She could make out only a few Seaponies in front of her. Somewhere in the distance, she heard Skystar's voice. "Fluttershy! Over here! Follow me!"

The only problem was, she couldn't figure out where "over here" was. Every time she swam one way, she'd notice a Seapony going in the opposite direction. Skystar had been in front of her for a while, but now Fluttershy didn't know where she'd gone. The sand and seaweed swirled all around them. It was impossible to tell where anypony was.

"Salt Air! Coral Rose!" Fluttershy called out into the deep. She waved her fin in front of her, trying to find her way through the water.

"Crystal Tide!" another Seapony called out. "Where are you? I can't see anything through the sand!"

"Stay in line!" Salt Air's voice said, but this time it was farther away.

Fluttershy spun around, trying to make out anypony in the dark. But now she couldn't see a single guard. They'd been traveling through the water for less than an hour, and they were already completely lost in the middle of a sandstorm.

Then, far out in the darkness, Fluttershy spotted a long, glowing orange light. It made *S* shapes in the water, moving up and down in front of her.

"Help is here!" an unfamiliar voice called.

"Follow this light over this way, yup, just like that! We're gonna lead you away from the sandstorm!"

Fluttershy did exactly what they said. The glowing orange light kept moving farther away, and Fluttershy kept following after it. It went a little to the right, and so did she. Within minutes she could see about a dozen Seaponies in front of her. The sand and seaweed in the water were mostly gone.

As she kept swimming forward, the water got clearer and clearer. Skystar and Salt Air emerged from the storm, too. When she swam closer to the light, she could see it wasn't a light at all, but some sort of orange eel floating next to a starfish with rainbow stripes.

"Is everypony out?" Salt Air said, glancing around at the group. "Is everypony safe?"

The rest of the Seaponies nodded. When they turned back, the storm was still swirling behind them. The water was a mess of sea plants and sand.

"The currents, you see—really bad currents," the rainbow starfish explained. "Creatures get caught up in there for days. Really a bit of a problem, but not one I can solve, no sirree. That sandstorm has been raging for as long as I've lived out here, yes that's right."

Fluttershy studied the creature. He was shorter than most starfish she'd seen in the village, with huge eyes that never looked directly at them. His middle was round and plump, and he had long, colorful stripes down his entire body. They went from fiery red to a deep purple, just like the rainbow.

"*Ummm…*" Skystar said, glancing around. "I don't mean to be rude, but who are you?"

"He's the starfish who just saved your tails!" the orange eel said. She squiggled toward them in an *S*, moving closer. She had a small, angry face and a tuft of white hair on the front of her head. Her voice was three octaves higher than any Fluttershy had heard before.

"Do me a favor, Harry," the eel said as she glided past Salt Air. "Next time you need me to save some creatures from the sandstorm, make sure they're the type to say 'thanks.'"

Then the eel shot out into the water, swimming fast in the opposite direction.

"Thank you!" Fluttershy called after her. But the eel was already far away, just a speck of light in the deep sea.

"I'm Harry, but I guess you already know that," the starfish said. "Lived out here my whole life. You must be the Seaponies; I can tell by your pony faces and the fins and everything. I've heard about you, yes, definitely heard a lot about you."

Seeing her chance, Fluttershy swam out in front of Salt Air to talk to the starfish. The last thing they needed was for Salt Air to scare Harry off, too.

"We're on a quest to find our friend Cerulean," she said. "She's also a Seapony. Have you seen her?"

"Can't say I have...but the crabs might know," Harry replied. He thought about it for a second and echoed the statement. "Yes, find the crabs."

"The crabs?" Fluttershy asked. She couldn't

help feeling a little excited at the prospect of meeting even more new creatures. "Who are they?"

"Chatty crabs, always yapping," Harry said. "Yappity yap yap yap. Follow me."

As Harry marched forward into the ocean, Fluttershy turned to see what the rest of the Seaponies thought. They all looked pleased that they'd found a creature who knew where they were and where they were going. Maybe Harry was a bit odd, but he had saved them. That counted for a lot.

They all followed. After a few minutes they came to a coral reef that was striped with the same rainbow pattern that covered Harry. Coral Rose swam beside Fluttershy. "None of this is on the map," she said, holding it in her fins. "I'll make sure I copy it down. The sandstorm was right here, and now I think we're right here." She pointed to two different places on the scroll.

They swam through the center of the reef, and the coral rose up on either side of them. Harry looked around and smiled. "Got some Seaponies here who are looking for the chatty crabs. Anyfish know where the chatty crabs have been hanging out, doing their yapping?"

He stared out at the coral. Fluttershy was confused. Was he talking to himself? Was he completely crazy? Who did he think would answer the question?

But suddenly a voice called out from the other side of the reef. "About fifty yards north! In the valley!"

Fluttershy watched as part of the coral moved, pointing them in the right direction. It took a minute for her eyes to adjust, but when she looked closely, she could see that the coral was covered with starfish just like Harry. They were all stuck to the sides of it, their bodies molded to the reef.

"You heard 'em," Harry said, pointing one of his arms in the same direction. "The crabs are thataway! Just tell them where you're going, and they'll help you. But they may chat your ears off first, you know."

Salt Air swam past, not bothering to say anything else to Harry. She waved the other Seaponies along behind her. They re-formed their line and started off. Fluttershy was the only one who turned back to Harry as they left.

"We won't forget what you did for us," she said. "Queen Novo will know that you and your friend are heroes."

For the first time since they met, Harry

looked directly at her. His eyes were big and watery, filled with rainbow tears. He smiled. "Just wanted to help out, you know, that's me, like to help!"

"Well, you certainly did!" Fluttershy agreed, giving him a smile that could light up the whole ocean. As Fluttershy swam off to join the others, she marveled at the sight of the beautiful rainbow starfish retreating behind her. The ocean certainly had its own special magic. But some things, such as kindness and gratitude, meant the same thing everywhere. If only Salt Air could realize it, too.

CHAPTER SIX

Fluttershy heard the chatty crabs before she saw them. Their voices carried through the water. One was talking about her friend Carol, and how she never used her pincers when she ate. The crab thought it was rude. "I just can't look at her when she does it," the crab said. "How am I supposed to enjoy my SnailMix when hers is all over her mouth?"

"What is that strange rattling noise?"

Skystar asked, looking around in confusion. "Is that the crabs?"

"This way," Salt Air said, swimming up a large mound of sand. Fluttershy followed her and Skystar to the top of it. The valley stretched out below, filled with hundreds of crabs sitting in the sand, all deep in conversation. Fluttershy could hear a crowd of crabs right below who were debating about vacations in the kelp forest.

"Who would want to go to the kelp forest when you can go to the Blue Cove?" one crab asked. "The Blue Cove has one of the best restaurants in the whole ocean. Those lotus rolls are to die for."

Before Fluttershy could say anything, Salt Air growled in frustration. "What was that starfish talking about?" She furrowed her brow, annoyed. "These crabs don't even speak our language! How are they of use to our mission?"

"Actually," Fluttershy said, swimming over to Salt Air, "I can understand them." On land, Fluttershy had the most amazing ability to communicate with creatures. Fortunately, it appeared to be the same down here.

"You can?!" Skystar's face exploded into a huge grin. "That is so super cool. Gosh, my friend is so cool!" Skystar nudged Coral Rose and pointed to Fluttershy. "That's my friend Fluttershy. Isn't she cool?"

"Princess," Salt Air said, interrupting Skystar's excited babble. "If these crabs can't help us, we really must keep moving—"

"You must be looking for that Seapony!" a crab with a spotted blue shell shouted. It just sounded like a rattling noise to the Seaponies. Everypony looked to Fluttershy.

"You saw Cerulean?" Fluttershy replied, eyes widening. Finally, another clue!

"Two days ago," the spotted blue crab said.

"Oh, I think it was yesterday, June," another crab chimed in.

"No, it wasn't! I know the days," the spotted blue crab replied, looking a little hurt.

"What are they saying?!" Skystar asked, almost bubbling over.

"Let's get the information and move on!" Salt Air begged.

Fluttershy sighed. "They're arguing about when they saw Cerulean pass by. I'm going to see if anycrab else knows something." One group was now discussing Sand Dragons and how old they actually were. Two crabs thought it was two thousand moons ago, while others thought it was two moons ago. Fluttershy didn't bother correcting them. Clearly, crabs had a very different sense of time than Seaponies. But Salt Air was growing impatient.

"Excuse me?" Fluttershy said, swimming toward a quieter group. They were saying something about the current weather. "You have quite a beautiful valley here. I was hoping you could just point us in the direction of the Sand Dragons' burrows," Fluttershy prodded. "Is it nearby?"

A crab's beady eyes darted around to his friends. He was neon yellow, with a red racing stripe across his back. He paused, as if considering whether she was worth helping, then he pointed across the valley with his biggest claw. "If you just go straight, you'll get to a tunnel. Go through it and out the other side, then you'll be there. I think that's where they are. But it's just a theory. Just watch out for the oogle worms."

"Oogle worms?" Fluttershy repeated for clarification. "Why should I watch out?"

"Oh, you'll see," another crab called out, then giggled as if he knew a big secret and wasn't telling.

Fluttershy smiled. She glanced over her shoulder at the other Seaponies, who were all gathered together, looking nervous as they watched the crabs. Coral Rose almost got her tail pinched!

"Thanks so much," Fluttershy said, giving the crabs a little bow. Then she called out to the guards. "I have another clue! Follow me!"

She swam across the valley, over packs of

chatty crabs, to where the yellow crab had pointed. The guards followed close behind, but Salt Air kept going out in front of her. It was clear she wanted to lead.

Within minutes Fluttershy spotted the tunnel entrance. It was a dark cavern in the sand. "That's it!" she said, turning to the others. "He said we just have to watch out for the oogle worms...."

"Oogle worms?" Coral Rose asked. Fluttershy just shrugged. She didn't know what they were, either.

"I'll take the lead," Salt Air called out, charging into the tunnel. "Be ready in case the beast appears!" She had her spear and shell shield raised, ready to fight. Now that they were close to the supposed Sand Dragons' territory, she seemed even more determined. Fluttershy was nervous again, thinking of what the Seapony might do once the group got there.

Fluttershy, Skystar, and Coral Rose all swam into the tunnel behind Salt Air. The rest of the guards trailed after them. It was completely dark. They hadn't gotten more than a few tail-spans inside and already Fluttershy couldn't see a thing.

"I'm here," Salt Air's voice was echoing up ahead. "Just keep swimming through."

Fluttershy felt a warm fin on her shoulder.

"I've got you," Skystar whispered to her. "Don't you worry!"

Fluttershy smiled, thinking of her friend beside her. Maybe it was dark, but if they stuck together they'd make it out okay. There was nothing to be afraid of.

They kept going, swimming as far and as

fast as they could. Finally, they saw the end of the tunnel. Fluttershy could just make out Salt Air up ahead. She swam out of the tunnel first, then Fluttershy followed her. She was about to cheer when she realized something had gone awry. Salt Air was waving her fins and spinning around and around in circles.

"What are they?!" she called out. *"Ooo.... grrr...."*

Three short, fat worms were coiled around her forelegs. They were black with bright-green polka dots and tiny, strange faces. They slunk across her shoulders, getting closer to her helmet.

Fluttershy reached up and touched her own shoulder, feeling an oogle worm there. What she'd thought were Skystar's fins had actually been worms—two of them.

She swam in quick circles, trying to get them off, but they clung to her. She had to dive into the sand to get rid of them.

When she finally emerged, all the Seaponies were frantically trying to get rid of their own oogle worms. Salt Air yanked off her helmet and pulled one out of it. Coral Rose was unraveling one that had curled around her neck. It took a few minutes, and some of the guards had to dive into the sand, but soon all the oogle worms were off them. The black-and-green creatures slunk back into the tunnel. Fluttershy swore one stuck out its tongue at her as it went, but maybe she was imagining things.

"That was revolting!" Skystar yelled. "But kinda fun in a weird way?!" She was brushing at her forelegs and tail, as if the worms were still there. A group of the Seaponies was still swimming in circles, grunting and groaning. "That must be why they call them oogle worms—that's the sound everypony makes when they're trying to get them off."

"It was on my neck!" a big, beefy Seapony whined. He shivered, as if he could still feel it there. *"Grrrr. . . ."* he cried.

Fluttershy looked above them, noticing where they were. Suddenly she didn't care about the tunnel or the chatty crabs or the oogle worm slime left on her shoulder. "Look!" Fluttershy cried out, pointing up at something she never thought she'd actually see. It was a real, gigantic Sand Dragon! It was instantly recognizable by its massive size, majestic fins, and grainy, sand-hued camouflage hide. Strangely enough, Fluttershy wasn't scared of it. The creature didn't seem dangerous at all. It looked gentle and somehow sad.

But Salt Air didn't notice any of that. All she saw was a monster.

"In formation!" Salt Air called out. The guards formed a triangle behind her, their spears pointed out. They swam forward, moving between the kelp.

"No, wait!" Fluttershy was right behind them with Skystar and Coral Rose. Glitterfish darted through the kelp, turning this way and that. Was Salt Air about to make everything worse?

"I am not afraid of Sand Dragons. I am not afraid of Sand Dragons..." Coral Rose whispered to herself as they got closer, her eyes squeezed shut.

Fluttershy swam as fast as she could to the front of the group. She held up her fin to stop them.

"Please," she said to Salt Air. "Let me talk to him first."

"You want to face a Sand Dragon alone?" Salt Air asked, glancing over her shoulder. "Have you been drinking seawater?"

"I know it sounds crazy," Fluttershy said. "But you have to give me the chance."

"A chance to make friends with"—Salt Air narrowed her eyes—"an ancient monster who wants to *eat* Seaponies?"

"A chance to get to Cerulean peacefully," Fluttershy said, "without raising a spear against an innocent creature."

Salt Air turned back to the other Seaponies. She tilted her head to the side as she considered it. Salt Air looked to Skystar. "And you're okay with this plan, Princess?" she asked.

"Absolutely!" Skystar said without hesitation.

"I trust Fluttershy. She knows more about creatures than anypony in Equestria!" The princess gave her friend a hopeful look. "I don't see why it should be any different with a Sand Dragon. I mean, the filly can talk to crabs!"

"We will try it your way first," Salt Air conceded, and motioned to her guards to retreat. She called out to Fluttershy. "But we will be right here, hiding in the forest. Just yell if you are in danger. We'll be ready."

The rest of the Seaponies nodded. Fluttershy turned back to the burrow and slowly swam out of the kelp forest toward the target. The Sand Dragon spotted her instantly. Suddenly, he didn't look so cute or sad anymore. He stalked forward, baring his horrible fangs.

"Is it finally time to eat?!" the Sand Dragon called out with a roar. His nostrils flared.

Fluttershy swallowed hard. *I am not afraid of Sand Dragons*, she thought. But as she stared up at the hideous creature, she realized how little she actually knew about this massive, mythical ocean beast. What had she gotten herself into?

CHAPTER SEVEN

I'm not here to cause any trouble," Fluttershy said, voice steady. "I can't find my friend Cerulean. I'm looking for her. Can you help?" She smiled her biggest, brightest smile, hoping it might charm the Sand Dragon, but his expression was fixed in a frown.

"Well, I can't find my family!" The Sand Dragon stalked around her. Most creatures under the water seemed weightless, but the Sand Dragon clomped around as if he were made of stone. With each hard step, he kicked up sand and shells. Fluttershy had to keep moving her wings around to keep the debris out of her face. "And even the Beezlebugs have abandoned me! How am I supposed to feast now?" the Sand Dragon growled.

Fluttershy gulped. "B-b-beezlebugs? I know where—"

"So what if I kept one of your Seaponies?" the Sand Dragon interrupted, and leaned in to Fluttershy's face. Up close, she could see that his teeth were the color of bananas. But to be fair, they hadn't been brushed in hundreds of moons. "I was all alone out here, what did you expect? A Sand Dragon can go crazy by himself, you know." He sighed. "I just wanted to talk to her...."

"Wait!" Fluttershy held up her fins. "So you didn't want to eat Cerulean?"

"Did she just say he ate Cerulean?!" a guard yelled out.

"Nooo!" Immediately, Salt Air snapped into action, motioning to the Seaponies to charge. Unfortunately, Fluttershy was still in the way. Most of the Seaponies stopped, unwilling to accidentally hurt her. But Salt Air was determined. She swam forward and lodged her spear into the Sand Dragon's tail.

"What are you doing?!" Fluttershy cried, but it was too late.

The Sand Dragon snarled. Then he whipped around. His giant tail flew so close to Salt Air's head she had to duck to avoid being hit. The Sand Dragon pushed through the sand and dove below, taking Fluttershy with him. The shouts of the guards above faded as they swam deep into the sand.

Everything was dark inside the sand burrow. It was lit only by a few eels who glided along the ceiling, casting long, creepy shadows on the walls. Fluttershy had been in scary places before, but nothing like this. It was worse than she'd imagined. Sea spiders peeked out from its nooks and caverns, as if they might swarm her at any moment.

Cerulean sat in front of her, her fins tied together with long pieces of kelp.

"Fluttershy?" Cerulean asked, perking up. "Where's Salt Air? Please tell me she didn't do anything rash—"

"She jabbed the Sand Dragon with her spear," Fluttershy exclaimed. "He was only trying to explain his woes to me, and she misheard. Are you okay?"

Cerulean nodded, but she looked quite shaken. Fluttershy wanted to ask her more, but then she heard the loud, clomping steps of the Sand Dragon coming toward her.

The Sand Dragon appeared in the far doorway, crying and clutching his tail in his claws. He lumbered over to a big chair nearby and plopped down. As soon as he sat down, he let out a horrible roar. It blew back Fluttershy's wings and shook the walls of the burrow. The spear was still stuck in his tail.

"At least I have another Seapony friend now," he cried out through his sobs. "Let me guess . . . you don't have anything to eat, either." At this, a loud rumble came from his tummy. He put his claw on it, embarrassed.

"Just some seaweed cake," Fluttershy replied, digging around in her bag until she found it.

The Sand Dragon perked up. "Did you say 'sea-weed'? How did you know that's my favorite?!"

"I didn't. But it's pretty much all the Seaponies like to eat, too," she explained. "Everywhere you go in Seaquestria, there's more seaweed to eat!"

The Sand Dragon narrowed his eyes. "So that's where all the food has gone?"

Cerulean could see that Fluttershy was having trouble putting it all together. "The seaweed fields are bare," she explained. "Usually, when Gnash and his buddies wake up from their hibernation, the Beezlebugs harvest the seaweed fields for them. They have a big feast together to regain their strength to spend a whole moon above the sands."

"Wow!" Fluttershy gasped, taking it all in. "That's a very different idea from what the Seaponies think...."

Gnash frowned. "What do they think?"

"Oh...well..." Fluttershy almost didn't want to tell him the horrible things she had heard the guards saying earlier. "That Sand Dragons rip apart starfish for fun? That you floss your fangs with stolen pony hair? That you, um...stomp around the sea looking for crabs to crunch?"

"But I don't do any of those things!" he cried out in despair. "It's not fair!"

"No," Fluttershy admitted, feeling sad for him. "It isn't. But lots of creatures are afraid of what they don't understand. If you let me and Cerulean go back to our kind, we can explain everything to them." Fluttershy looked at up him with sympathetic eyes. "And then they won't be scared anymore!"

Gnash considered this. He paced in front of her, then dropped back onto his front legs. "They wouldn't try to spear me again?"

"No, they wouldn't," Fluttershy agreed. "This has all been one big misunderstanding. And it needs to be resolved right now."

"Okay, but they have to leave the Beezle-bug fields alone!" Gnash cried out, seemingly out of nowhere. His nostrils flared. He started breathing heavily, as if he was so angry he might explode. "And where are my friends and family? I can't find any of their burrows! Everything is different up there now with this Seapony kingdom built on our land."

"We didn't know it was their land," Cerulean shot back. "Their burrows are underground."

"We should knock it all down!" Gnash suggested.

"You will not!" Cerulean said, an edge to her voice. "We have built our whole lives there!"

Fluttershy couldn't take it any longer. The

way things were going, they'd be arguing for another century.

"If the Sand Dragons build their homes under-ground," Fluttershy tried, "then you can't blame the Seaponies for not knowing where they were. After all, they are new to Seaquestria. They haven't been here for centuries like you have."

Gnash didn't respond. He seemed as if he was listening, but Fluttershy couldn't be sure. He snarled again, letting out a flurry of bubbles.

"And just think about why they left Mount Aris—their home was destroyed by their enemy," she continued. "How do you think they'd feel if you threatened to destroy their *new* home?"

"The same way I felt when I woke up to find that everything had changed," Gnash said, annoyed. "Terrible."

"Exactly," Fluttershy said. "Why don't you try to become friends with one another? Teach them what land is Sand Dragon territory. You can work together to harvest the seaweed fields—that way no Seapony, Sand Dragon, or Beezlebug will go hungry again!"

"I'm so hungry!" Gnash roared. Fluttershy passed him another seaweed cake and floated quietly. She waited, watching as Gnash ate the treat and slowly calmed down. It took him a minute to absorb what she'd said, but he seemed to understand. "Now I can think."

"Does that sound okay to you?" Fluttershy asked, looking to Cerulean.

"It does," the Seapony agreed. "We have yet to explore a lot of the sea. It would be an honor to have you show us more about our new home in the ocean. We can help you find your other sand burrows. And maybe we could even make a few giant-size seaweed cakes that the Sand Dragons can enjoy once they wake up...."

Gnash glanced at the spear in his tail. "And no more spears?"

"Of course not!" Cerulean said, looking a bit embarrassed. "We will even help you remove that one."

"Okay, then," Gnash agreed. He untied the kelp around Cerulean's fins and sighed. "I guess you two can go...." He slumped down, looking sad. "But I hope you do come back."

"Friends don't let one another down!" Fluttershy replied without missing a beat. "We'll see you soon. Let's not wait any longer. Salt Air must be quite scared by now...."

Gnash nodded and opened the door to release Fluttershy and Cerulean. They swam in circles, relieved to be free again. Cerulean spread her fins and did a quick, joyful spin.

Fluttershy swam forward, about to thank Gnash and Cerulean for their understanding, when she heard something behind her. She turned to see Salt Air hovering in the main burrow. Her face was lit up by the glow of the electric eels. The Seaponies were right behind her, their spears aimed at Gnash!

Fluttershy's heart sank. They had come to fight. Before she could stop them, the Seaponies charged forward.

"Attack!" Salt Air yelled. Then she launched another spear, hurling it toward Gnash's head.

CHAPTER EIGHT

Gnash dove out of the way. As he did, his front leg swung to the side, knocking Cerulean into the wall. She hit the stone hard and slumped against it. Two guards swam to her and held her, trying to wake her up.

"Stop this!" Fluttershy called out, but nocreature could hear her over the *clash* and *clank* of the spears.

Gnash rammed against Coral Rose's shell

shield, sending the Seapony flying back. The Sand Dragon bit down on a guard's spear and snapped it in half. "You promised no more spears! You lied!"

Fluttershy swam to the ceiling, trying to get Salt Air's attention, but the Seapony was calling out orders to the rest of the guards. She didn't even look up.

"Salt Air—over here!" Cerulean yelled, trying to distract her. Gnash was already fighting six Seaponies at once. They kept charging him with their spears, but they were hardly a match for the giant beast. As each one sped forward, the Sand Dragon knocked them away. One Seapony hit the wall. Another was thrown backward into two other guards. Salt Air snuck up behind the Sand Dragon, but he turned and roared loudly in her face. A rush of bubbles came out of his mouth and pinned her to the floor.

The more times the Seaponies got knocked down, the more desperate Fluttershy became to put a stop to the madness. She couldn't stand the thought of Gnash getting hurt again. Fluttershy swam over to Gnash and spread her fins out wide in front of him. Immediately, everycreature froze.

"Please, Salt Air! Listen to me!" she cried. "He didn't want to eat Cerulean! He didn't even hurt her! All he wanted was some seaweed to eat and to find his friends!"

Fluttershy saw Princess Skystar in the corner of the burrow. She looked frustrated. Her guards were on either side of her, trying to protect her from the fight.

That was it! Fluttershy swam over. If anypony could control Salt Air, it would be Skystar.

"Skystar!" she said. "Order them to stop!

Tell them there's been a misunderstanding. The Sand Dragons are gentle creatures. They don't even crunch crabs!"

"I thought as much!" Skystar's eyes darted to Salt Air, who was still trying to fight. Skystar's eyes narrowed in a mixture of determination and anger. "Why are they doing this?" she asked. Nopony answered. "My mother didn't order an attack on a peaceful creature!"

Two Seapony guards circled Gnash, each darting behind him. He kept swatting them away, but two more showed up after them. A pink Seapony with huge purple wings zig-zagged behind him, then landed a quick blow with her shield, hitting him in the back.

Skystar knew that Fluttershy was right. If she wanted the battle to stop, she'd have to stop it herself. Three guards were closing in on Gnash.

She swam down, putting herself between them and him. She held up both of her fins.

"As princess of Seaquestria, I order you to stop!" she yelled as the Seaponies raced toward her. "Queen Novo does not want this. This is all a mistake."

The three Seaponies slowed down, floating just in front of her. One flipped up her helmet. "A mistake?" she asked. "What do you mean?"

"This Sand Dragon didn't hurt anypony," Fluttershy explained. "It's the Seaponies who owe him an apology for building on top of the Sand Dragons' ancient burrows and harvesting all the seaweed!"

The Seaponies glanced around, waiting for Salt Air to respond to the claim.

"But he ponynapped Cerulean!" Salt Air swam forward. "No gentle creature would take a hostage like that. He's just trying to trick us!" She held her spear up and aimed it right at Gnash's belly. "I'm sorry, Fluttershy."

Fluttershy watched as the Sand Dragon closed his eyes, scared of what would come next. She couldn't take it any longer. As Salt Air hurled the spear, Fluttershy shot out toward it, swimming as fast as she could. She put herself between them, crashing into the coral spear before it could hit him. The spear flew off course and went right past Gnash's shoulder. But Fluttershy was moving so fast she couldn't stop herself. She swam straight into the side of the burrow, crashing headfirst. She felt a heavy, spinning feeling, and then everything went dark.

CHAPTER NINE

"Fluttershy?" a voice said softly. "Fluttershy, can you hear me?"

Fluttershy's eyes were closed. She could tell something was going on around her, but she couldn't tell what. Her head was throbbing. Where was she? How long had she been here? And did she really have to wake up? Wherever she was, this bed was so cozy and warm....

"Fluttershy?" the voice said again.

Fluttershy slowly opened her eyes. She was in a room she'd never seen before. It looked like the Sand Dragon's burrow, because it had the same gray walls and seaweed curtains that were in the great hall. Electric eels lined the ceiling, snaking this way and that, lighting up everything with their orange glow.

"She's awake!" Princess Skystar cried. "Fluttershy! Fluttershy! Are you okay?"

Fluttershy looked down, noticing the bed she'd been sleeping in. It was a mixture of moss and sea sponge. They'd covered her with a thick blanket made of kelp. Her head still hurt, and she was sore, but other than that, she felt okay.

"I think so..." Fluttershy said. She looked around at all the worried faces. Gnash was standing beside Skystar. As soon as he saw her eyes open, he smiled a big, toothy grin, revealing a row of yellow and brown fangs. Salt Air and the guards stood on the far side of the room. Cerulean and Coral Rose both hung their heads. They didn't look at her.

"Thank my lucky starfish!" Skystar said with a giggle. Then she grew serious. "Salt Air and the guards know now they cannot act without my permission. What they did tonight was, like, completely inexcusable, you know?"

"Your Highness," Salt Air said, still keeping her eyes on the floor, "again, I beg your forgiveness. We thought the Sand Dragon had captured Cerulean and Fluttershy. We thought we needed to do something. To rescue them and prevent Seaquestria from a Sand Dragon attack!"

"You could have really hurt Gnash," Skystar said. "And for what? Because you were angry?

Because you assumed the worst? Because you didn't listen?"

Salt Air didn't answer.

Princess Skystar swam toward her, shaking her head. "You could learn something from Fluttershy! We all could."

Salt Air laughed. "From the same pony who tried to steal the pearl? Didn't her friend run off with it when you weren't looking?"

"Um, *nooooo*. From the same pony who *stood up to you* when no other pony would!" Skystar corrected. "And will you let that pearl thing go already? I think she proved she's on our side here tonight!"

Gnash paced beside Fluttershy's bed. His scaly skin was scratched up in a few places, but otherwise, he seemed okay. He stared at Salt Air, his dark brows pulled together. "I should take you as my prisoner!" he joked. When nopony laughed, he just shrugged. "What? Too soon?"

Skystar stifled a giggle. Salt Air looked particularly salty about the comment.

Gnash plopped down beside Fluttershy's bed, and a small smile crept over his face. He suddenly seemed calmer and maybe even... happy. Fluttershy was starting to think he was like a lot of creatures she'd met on her adventures—all roar and no bite. It didn't seem as if Gnash actually wanted to hurt anycreature, even if they were trying to hurt him.

"You are a nice Seapony," Gnash said, gazing at Fluttershy. "I've never seen bravery like that. And I've been alive for five hundred moons! You risked your life for a stranger, and for a stranger who accidentally ponynapped your friend. If the Beezlebugs were here, they would present you with a heaping plate of seaweed mash as a thank-you."

"It was the right thing to do," Fluttershy said, and she meant every word. Maybe Gnash had made some mistakes, and maybe he did have a fiery temper, but that didn't mean Salt Air was allowed to hurt him. What kind of pony would Fluttershy be if she had stood frozen, watching the battle? She couldn't have lived with herself if anypony or anydragon was hurt... or worse.

"Gnash," Skystar started, "I want you to know that no matter what happened tonight, you can count the Seaponies as friends. We're sorry for all these misunderstandings and for not finding you sooner. When you're moving thousands of Hippogriffs under the ocean, you can sometimes forget your manners."

Gnash's eyes darted to the back wall where Cerulean and Salt Air were still standing. His expression grew serious again. He kept looking at Skystar, then back to the Seaponies, as if he wasn't sure whom to trust.

"Skystar never says anything that she doesn't mean," Fluttershy assured him. "Please, give the Seaponies another chance."

"She's right! Tomorrow night we will be back in the village," Skystar went on. "And we will hold a ball in your honor. With a feast! Please come as our special guest! Oh, you just have to!"

"You all want me there?" Gnash glanced around the room. The Seaponies' expressions began to change from solemn to smiles. "You're sure that's a good idea?" Gnash asked. "I thought that Seaponies hated me. That they thought I was a"—he paused, as though he couldn't bring himself to say it—"crab-cruncher."

"We will explain everything," Fluttershy said. She turned to the guards. "Right, everypony?"

"*Hmmm*…what would I even wear?" Gnash asked. "I mean, I haven't been to a ball in… well, ever."

"Wear whatever you like!" Skystar said. "You can meet my mom, Queen Novo, and some of the villagers!" The princess leaned in and gave him a little wink. "I think some of your friends might be in attendance as well."

"Really?!" Gnash smiled a big, goofy smile, as if he'd been trying to hold it back but couldn't. Then he returned to his seat beside Fluttershy. "You can stay here to recover if you need to," he said. "There's a good glitterfish doctor a few miles west. Well, at least there was a hundred moons ago...."

But Fluttershy was already up. She pushed back the kelp blanket and swam into the room. Her head still felt a little heavy, but otherwise, she was okay. "I'm all right, I think. I can go back with them," she said. "Besides, I'm sure Queen Novo is worried about you, Skystar. I'm sure she's worried about all of us."

Fluttershy bowed in front of the giant beast, and he bowed back.

"It was an honor," he said in that gentler tone that seemed to come and go.

"We will see you tomorrow night at the ball," Skystar said as her guards formed two lines around her. Fluttershy stayed toward the back with Coral Rose, holding on to her wing in case she needed to steady herself.

"Tomorrow night!" Gnash called after them with another huge smile. As they filed out of the Sand Dragon's burrow, Fluttershy swore she could hear the beast giggling with excitement.

CHAPTER TEN

Skystar!" Queen Novo yelled from the upstairs window. She had been keeping lookout on the second floor of the castle, waiting for her daughter and the guards to return. As soon as she saw them coming up the street, she disappeared from her perch, then reappeared at the main gates. She swam as fast as she could toward them.

"You're home," she said, throwing her fins

around Skystar. She buried her face in her daughter's neck. "I was so worried. I heard the guards talking about the Sand Dragon, and how vicious it was, and—"

Skystar laughed. "Actually, I think he was just a little bit *hangry*, you know?"

"Hangry?" Queen Novo repeated.

"Like hungry and angry at the same time," Skystar replied. *"Moooom. It's slang!"*

Queen Novo nodded, looking confused. "Oh. Right."

Skystar continued. "But anyway, we worked through the misunderstanding, thanks to my best friend Fluttershy!" Skystar said, darting over to Fluttershy and giving her the biggest hug.

Fluttershy tried to smile, but she could barely breathe. Skystar was squeezing her so tightly. *"Thanks . . ."* she barely got out.

"He didn't hurt you, did he?" Queen Novo asked, swimming around her daughter to check for scrapes or bumps. "The stories I was hearing had me so scared—"

"You'll meet him soon enough," Skystar said. "And you can see for yourself."

"What?" Queen Novo asked. "Skystar! What have you gone and done now?"

Skystar glanced over Queen Novo's head to the two Seaponies at the castle gate. "Tell the cooks to prepare a seaweed feast for tomorrow night! We're throwing one of the grandest balls Seaquestria has ever known, in honor of our new alliance with the Sand Dragon. Spare no expense!"

Queen Novo's eyes went wide. "The Sand Dragon is coming... *here*?"

"His name is Gnash, and he's going to be guest of honor," Fluttershy explained. "He really isn't as bad as everypony says. He's kind of nice sometimes. Did you know he's friends with the Beezlebugs?"

Skystar pointed to the square down below. Hundreds of the blue critters were still scrabbling around in the streets. "Well, then he should love it here!" They all laughed as Queen Novo called the rest of the guards from the mission back inside.

The Seaponies filed inside the great hall. Fluttershy had never been so happy to return somewhere. It was so different from the Sand Dragon's lair, with huge, open windows and light streaming in from every direction. One of the castle crabs was playing the harp, filling the entire room with peaceful music.

Skystar swam up and down, doing a few quick spins. "If the Sand Dragon is coming here for a ball, then I need a new gown and have to figure out how to do my mane, and we need to bring in flowers from the water poppy field!" She grabbed her pale-blue mane and lifted it up and down, then she pulled it to the side. "Updo or down? Side braid? I can't decide! Come on, Fluttershy, we have to find you the perfect look, too!"

Skystar grabbed Fluttershy's fin and pulled her toward the castle gates. They swam past Cerulean and Salt Air. Salt Air had barely said a word the entire journey back to the castle. But now she looked directly at Fluttershy, as if she wanted to say something. Fluttershy slowed down and pulled Skystar to a stop.

"I thought about it," Salt Air said, carefully choosing her words. "And Princess Skystar was right. I could learn a lot from what happened out there, and I could learn a lot from you. I shouldn't have attacked Gnash like that. I didn't even know him! My temper sometimes gets the better of me."

"I could tell," Fluttershy admitted. For everything everypony had said about the Sand Dragon, the scariest moment had been when Salt Air burst through the sand burrow without understanding the situation. Fluttershy felt helpless watching her charge at the Sand Dragon. She knew it was only making everything worse. "But I'm glad that you're finally ready to listen before judging new creatures." Fluttershy smiled. "It makes all the difference in the ocean!"

Cerulean nudged Salt Air in the side, urging her to say more.

"I also wanted to say," Salt Air added, "that… I'm sorry. And thanks. For everything."

Fluttershy reached out her fin, letting Salt Air take it. Salt Air had been so sure of herself and so sure Fluttershy was wrong. She'd acted as if Fluttershy was just another traitor coming to ruin Seaquestria. Fluttershy felt a sense of relief wash over her now that Salt Air knew the truth. She was only trying to help.

"Friends?" Fluttershy asked, reaching out her fin.

"Friends!" Salt Air agreed as she shook it.

"Come on!" Skystar yelled, swimming out ahead of her. "The shops are closing soon!"

With that, Fluttershy darted off, following her friend into the village.

Queen Novo flitted around the great hall, studying the bouquets of water poppies in the center of each table. She checked and double-checked the place settings and made sure the napkins were clean. Then she swam through the kitchens and sampled every dish the cooks had made. When she finally emerged, she was dabbing her mouth with her fin.

"They just turned the corner toward the castle!" Queen Novo shouted.

Fluttershy's ears were playing tricks on her. Had the queen just seen multiple Sand Dragons? "Excuse me, Your Majesty? Did you say '*they*'?"

"She did!" Skystar squealed in delight. She pointed out the window. Sure enough, Gnash was making his way through the village, followed by five other massive Sand Dragons. "It looks as if Gnash found his friends! And they're almost here!"

"Music, please!" Queen Novo called out.

A ten-piece band was floating in the corner of the room. A glitterfish was at the piano, and three blowfish were in the horn section, playing trumpets and tubas. A spotted crab was on the guitar. He counted the whole group off, and they burst into a lively song.

Fluttershy and Skystar leaned out the window, watching the scene outside. Hundreds of villagers had come out to see the huge Sand Dragons. Only this time, instead of yelling or chanting words against them, the Seaquestrians were quietly watching their every move. Some Seafoals smiled and waved. Others applauded as the Sand Dragons clomped by, their steps slow and heavy. The Beezlebugs fell in line beside them, carrying little pieces of seaweed in their claws. Queen Novo had ordered a dozen guards to bring them into the village, and they swam on either side of them, making sure they were safe.

"Who is that?" Queen Novo asked, pointing to the Sand Dragon in the back. "He certainly dressed up for the occasion."

Fluttershy swam to the next window to get a better view. There, at the back of the line of Sand Dragons, was Gnash. He must've spent hours getting ready. He was wearing a three-piece kelp-tweed suit and a top hat made of urchin shells. He'd even tucked a kerchief in his front pocket!

"That's Gnash!" Fluttershy said with a chuckle. "Wow, who would have guessed he had such great style?"

"That's a snazzy suit, yes, it is!" Princess Sky-star laughed.

Queen Novo threw open the front gates to welcome them. There were six Sand Dragons in all, and they were all in different outfits. One of the female Sand Dragons had on a long kelp gown with huge, poufy sleeves. Her sharp claws were painted with purple squid ink.

"Welcome to Seaquestria. Please, come in!" Queen Novo said. She gestured to the giant tables in the great hall. They'd cleared out a lot of the furniture so the huge Sand Dragons would have room to move around.

"Pleasure to see you again," Gnash said, offering the princess a little bow. "And this must be Queen Novo."

The queen gave a deep bow. "That's me! Thank you for agreeing to let us host and for...not eating us."

For a second, the entire great hall froze. Even the band stopped playing their music. Every-pony was worried about what Gnash would do. They couldn't have Sand Dragons losing their temper in the middle of the great hall.

After a long pause, Gnash just laughed. "Very funny!" he said, stomping his claw on the stone. "You're funny."

Queen Novo smiled, sharing a look with Fluttershy as the music began again.

There were more moments like that throughout the night, when everypony seemed unsure about Gnash and his friends. Were they about to lose their tempers and destroy the whole castle? Could they really be trusted?

But those moments always passed, and the answers eventually seemed clear. (No, they wouldn't destroy the castle. Yes, they could be trusted.) As Queen Novo held up her glass at the end of the night, it really did feel as if the Sand Dragons and Seaponies were becoming friends. Gnash had spent a good hour introducing each of the hundreds of Beezlebugs by name and title.

"To centuries of good will!" Queen Novo said, offering a toast.

"To centuries of good will!" the Sand Dragons called out.

"And to all the seaweed we can eat!" Skystar added, laughing. "I'm really looking forward to that!"

The whole room clinked glasses. Fluttershy smiled as she sipped her cider, happy she'd played some small part in it all.

"This was one of the most interesting days I've had in a *loooooong* time," Skystar said, giving her friend a hug.

"Really?" Fluttershy asked, hoping that was a good thing.

"Yeah!" Skystar said. "For once, I didn't make a single thing out of seashells...."

"Oh no, did you still want to do that?" Fluttershy said, pulling Skystar away from the dance floor. "Because there's still time if we—"

"No, silly!" Skystar giggled. "Who has time for shells when they've got a best friend to cut a rug with?! Come on!" The princess grabbed Fluttershy's fin, and they rushed back out into the middle of the floor.

When the band started a faster song, the two Seaponies twirled around in the water, dancing between the giant Sand Dragons, Queen Novo, the Beezlebugs, and the guards. For the first time in the history of Seaquestria, they were all together, and they were having fun— all because they were going with the flow of friendship.

TURN THE PAGE FOR A
SPECIAL PREVIEW OF

SEE HOW THE
STORY BEGAN!

AVAILABLE NOW

PROLOGUE

Tempest Shadow stood on the deck of the airship, looking down at Canterlot. The royal castle stood in the middle of the capital. She was hidden in the clouds high above. Nopony could see her. Nopony even knew she was there.

"It's an impressive city," she said, turning to Grubber. "But we have our chance. The Friendship Festival is happening soon."

"You think that would be a good time to steal the magic from the princesses?" Grubber asked. He sat next to her on the deck of the ship, talking in between bites of his muffin.

"The perfect time. We can descend from the airship to be safe," Tempest said. "There will be so many ponies in Canterlot during the festival, and everypony will be busy and having fun. We'll take them all by surprise."

"Genius plan," Grubber said.

"Now let's take one last look around. We should find out exactly where the entrance to the castle is, and what each of the princesses looks like. The more we know about Canterlot before the Friendship Festival, the better."

"But don't I need a disguise?" Grubber asked.

It felt like years since Tempest Shadow had met Grubber. The short, round creature was less than half her size, with a tuft of white hair and piercing blue eyes. She hadn't seen a creature like him before, in Equestria or anywhere else.

She grabbed two cloaks from the airship cabin and draped one over herself and one over Grubber. Then she ordered the ship down toward Canterlot. They'd dock on the outskirts of the city and make their way to the center. Who knew what they would find there . . . ?

CHAPTER ONE

The young Unicorn walked through the forest, her two best friends right beside her. Glitter Drops and Spring Rain were Unicorns, too, and together the three of them liked to practice their magic. Every morning they'd venture out into the forest or explore the mountains by their small town, taking a break now and then to play ball.

"There it is," the young Unicorn said as

they stepped into the clearing. She stared into the sky.

Canterlot was high above them. The capital of Equestria was perched in the mountains and could be seen for miles around. The three friends had never actually been there, but they'd heard hundreds of stories. The city was filled with ivory towers and waterfalls, shimmering spires and majestic views. Most important, it was the home of two of the three princesses, and a common spot for them to meet.

The three princesses were Alicorns, or Unicorns with powerful wings. Princess Celestia and Princess Luna controlled the sun and the moon, and Princess Cadance was the ruler of the Crystal Empire. She had been Princess Celestia's apprentice when she was younger.

"Do you think we'll ever get there?" Spring Rain asked.

"Of course we will," the young Unicorn said. "And who knows…"

Glitter Drops smiled. "Maybe one of us will become a princess one day, too."

"But first, Princess Celestia's School for Gifted Unicorns," the young Unicorn said. "Where all the most talented Unicorns learn to focus their powerful magic. We'll get there someday; I know we will."

The young Unicorn couldn't admit it to even her closest friends, but she thought about Princess Celestia's school every single day. She dreamed about studying in Canterlot, of learning to make magic that glowed and sparked with power. She'd work as hard as she could to make Princess Celestia proud. Sometimes she even imagined becoming an Alicorn herself. Would she ever be given wings? Could she ever be that powerful?

There were entrance exams every spring. The young Unicorn hoped she'd be ready when they came around one moon. She wanted to attend the school as soon as she could. It was hard waiting for something you wanted so much.

"Let's practice," she said, turning to Glitter Drops and Spring Rain. "Let's levitate the ball."

Glitter Drops's horn sparked and glowed. She took the ball from her satchel and sent it flying off into the woods. The young Unicorn darted after it, weaving in and out of the trees. She could just see the ball up ahead, glowing in the air. It was like the bouncy balls other ponies tossed back and forth, only this one was special. If she focused her magic, she could make it float and glow with a beautiful white light. It looked like the moon.

"I can't keep up!" Glitter Drops called out. She was running as fast as she could through the forest, but the ball was always a little ahead of her. She laughed as she ran, clearly loving the way the wind felt in her mane.

Spring Rain darted out in front of the young Unicorn. She raced across the ground to the ball, but she stumbled and fell. She hadn't been concentrating hard enough, but that wasn't her fault. It was tough to concentrate on her magic, run really fast, *and* keep her eyes on the ball.

The young Unicorn galloped out in front of both of her friends. The ball was up ahead.

She was so close. She just had to run a little faster....

"Where'd it go?" Spring Rain's voice called out. "It disappeared!"

The young Unicorn stopped at the mouth of a cave. The ball had floated inside. She could still see the glowing light, but it was dimmer now. The ball was somewhere in there, deep in the mountain.

"Oh no..." Glitter Drops stopped right behind her. She peered inside. The cave was so dark they couldn't see past the opening. "Who's going to go get it?"

Glitter Drops and Spring Rain turned to their brave friend. The purple Unicorn might've been the youngest, but she was always the bravest of the three. She'd talked to the hydra when they went to Froggy Bottom Bogg, and she had found her way through the Everfree Forest on her own. Whenever something scary happened, her friends always looked to her first.

"I'll be right back," the young Unicorn said. Then she ventured into the cave, trying to follow the dim light from the ball.

Inside, she could hardly see anything. The ball was somewhere up ahead, around a sharp corner, but she couldn't make out the floor of the cave. She stumbled over a rock and fell, landing hard. When she finally got up, her shoulder hurt.

"This isn't as easy as I thought it would be...." she said to herself, rubbing the sore spot on her side. She went slower now, being careful with each step. "Just a little farther...."

She was getting closer. As she turned the

corner, she saw the ball floating in the air. That whole part of the cave was lit up now. She could see everything perfectly.

It looked like some creature had been living there. There were scraps of food and a warm, cozy bed. She reached up, grabbed the ball, and tucked it behind her front leg. When she turned back around, there was an ursa minor standing right in front of her.

She didn't have time to react. The bear roared in her face. She ducked underneath its foreleg, trying to get away, but it chased after her. She didn't move more than a few feet before it struck her with its giant paw. She went flying across the cave, her head knocking into the wall.

She got up as fast as she could, knowing the bear would be right behind her. As she got closer to the entrance of the cave, she could see Glitter Drops and Spring Rain waiting for her. They were both staring inside the cave, trying to see what was happening.

"Run!" she yelled. "There's an ursa minor!"

Spring Rain and Glitter Drops turned around and darted off through the forest. The young Unicorn followed them, relieved when she was finally out of the cave. She'd dropped the ball at some point along the way, but it didn't matter. She had to get as far away from the ursa minor as she could.

She didn't stop running until she was out of the forest and saw Spring Rain and Glitter Drops standing in the field up ahead. She turned back, looking into the trees to make sure they were safe. After all that, they were finally alone. The bear hadn't followed them.

"I went all the way to the back of the cave," the young Unicorn said. "I found the ball, but then, when I turned around, the ursa minor was right behind me. It chased me, and then I fell, and then..."

Glitter Drops and Spring Rain just stared at her. Their eyes were wide, and their expressions were serious. They looked like something was horribly wrong. The young Unicorn glanced down at her hooves, making sure she wasn't hurt. She looked over her shoulder at her tail and mane. Everything seemed fine.

"I don't think I'm hurt," she said. "Just a few scratches..."

"I don't know how to tell you this...." Glitter Drops said, her eyes watering. "It's your horn."

The young Unicorn reached up and touched the front of her head. Her horn was just a small, jagged stump—the top half had broken off. Her eyes immediately filled with tears.

"No," she said, shaking her head. "No—it can't be. What's a Unicorn without her horn?"

"I'm so sorry." Glitter Drops hugged her friend.

"It'll be okay," Spring Rain added, wrapping her front leg around the young Unicorn's other side.

The tears streamed down the young Unicorn's cheeks. She'd lost her horn. All her magic was contained within it. How would anything ever be okay again?

CHAPTER TWO

The young Unicorn and her two friends set off through town, Spring Rain walking on one side of her and Glitter Drops walking on the other. She'd waited weeks, then months, for her horn to grow back, but nothing had happened. This was the first time she'd left her house since the day at the cave, but Spring Rain and Glitter Drops had told her it would be okay. She still couldn't help but feel nervous, though. Every time she looked at her broken horn she started crying.

She'd pulled a hat down over her head, and nopony seemed to notice anything was different. She waved at everypony inside the market, and everypony waved back. They passed their friend Moonglow, who was planting tulips outside the art gallery.

"What a lovely hat!" Moonglow said. "The flowers on it are beautiful."

"Thank you, Moonglow," the young Unicorn called as she trotted past.

"See?" Glitter Drops asked. "Is it really that bad?"

The young Unicorn shook her head. "You were right. It feels good to be out and about."

As they got to the clearing, Spring Rain

looked around and took a ball out of her satchel. There weren't many ponies near them. "Want to try it?" she asked. "It couldn't hurt...."

At first the young Unicorn wasn't sure what she was talking about. But then Spring Rain lifted the ball a few inches off the ground, levitating it in front of her.

"Oh, no...I shouldn't," the young Unicorn said. "I haven't used my horn for magic since the accident. I don't even know if it'll work."

"You're the bravest Unicorn we know," Glitter Drops said. "I always tell stories about my friend who isn't afraid of anypony or anything. You can do whatever you put your mind to."

The young Unicorn glanced back toward town. There wasn't anypony around. Maybe it wouldn't be the worst thing to just try. She hadn't had the courage to since her horn broke.

"Ready?" Spring Rain said, dropping the ball back to the ground.

The young Unicorn nodded and took off her hat. Glitter Drops and Spring Rain both trotted out in front of her, farther into the clearing. She focused her magic on her horn, trying to lift the ball off the ground. Her horn sparked. She stood there, waiting for it to work as a few more sparks shot out toward the trees.

Her power was building—she could feel it—and suddenly her broken horn shot off an incredible show of light. It was burning hot, and turned everything it touched to ash and dust. A whole row of trees burned underneath it.

"Watch out!" Glitter Drops cried as the

young Unicorn stepped forward, trying to control it. She stumbled, and as her head turned, she scorched a patch of grass.

When her horn finally stopped shooting sparks, she stood there, trying to catch her breath. Spring Rain was lying in the grass. She'd bumped her head. Glitter Drops was hiding behind a tree. The young Unicorn reached out her hoof to help Spring Rain stand, but her friend flinched. When she stared up at her, her eyes were full of fear.

"I didn't mean it," the young Unicorn tried to explain. "I don't know what happened. . . ."

Spring Rain stood on her own. She brushed herself off and offered her friend a small smile. "It's okay. It was an accident."

Glitter Drops came up next to them, but the young Unicorn noticed both her friends didn't get too close. They kept glancing at her horn. They seemed afraid of her now. "Are you okay?" Glitter Drops asked Spring Rain. "That was a serious fall."

"I think I'm all right.... It was just scary," Spring Rain said.

"I'm so sorry," the young Unicorn said. "It's something about my horn.... It doesn't work right anymore."

"It's okay," Spring Rain said again, but she seemed sad. "Let's just go back home."

Glitter Drops and Spring Rain turned back toward town, and all the young Unicorn could do was follow. She knew Spring Rain was just frightened, but she couldn't help feeling like everything was her fault. Her horn was broken, her magic was gone, and things would never be the same between them. Everything had gone so wrong after that day at the cave.

She walked beside her friends, her hat snug on her head again. Glitter Drops and Spring Rain didn't say anything else. The young Unicorn's mind was racing: Would she ever get her magic back? How would her friends be able to trust her? And how could she stay in her town when everything felt so wrong?

CHAPTER THREE

The moons passed. The young Unicorn spent more and more time at home, reading and baking and doing anything that didn't remind her of the magic she'd once had. Glitter Drops and Spring Rain still came by to see her every once in a while, but they never asked her to go to the clearing with them to practice magic. They never even mentioned her horn. Instead they pretended as if that day in the cave had never happened.

So when they knocked on her door one morning, she hoped maybe something had changed. Maybe they weren't afraid of her after all.

She flung open the door.

"Where to?" she asked. She'd already put on her hat. It had been so long since she'd seen her friends; she couldn't help but miss them and all the fun times they'd had. She'd just go with them to get some apple cider, and then she'd come home. She wouldn't even talk about magic or what they used to do in the clearing.

"Actually…" Glitter Drops began slowly. She looked a little sad. "We wanted to talk to you about something."

"What do you mean?" the young Unicorn asked.

"We took the entrance exams for Princess Celestia's School for Gifted Unicorns," Spring Rain said. "We wanted to tell you before you heard it from any other pony."

The young Unicorn tried to hide the hurt in her expression, but she could already feel her eyes welling up with tears. Since the day she'd broken her horn, she'd tried to bury her dreams down deep in her heart. She hoped that one day her horn would grow back, along with her magic, and she could go to Princess Celestia's school, but until then she tried her best to forget. Sometimes she wouldn't even glance up at Canterlot. It was hard to see the city glittering in the sky and not think of all the possibilities of a future there.

"I didn't realize they'd happened already," the young Unicorn said. "I just...I hadn't thought about it since..."

"We know," Glitter Drops said. "And we know your horn is going to grow back soon. It's only a matter of time. But we felt like we had to take the exams this moon. The term starts in the fall."

"So you're going?" she asked as she tried to steady her voice.

"Yeah," Spring Rain said. "But you'll come next moon. We'll all be together again soon. And we'll come back to visit all the time. We'll still be friends."

"Right," the young Unicorn said. "Of course. We'll always be friends. I'm happy for you."

The young Unicorn put on her best smile, even though she was hurting. Glitter Drops and Spring Rain looked relieved that she was being so nice about it. She said good-bye to her friends, and they promised that they'd see one another the next day. She told them they were going to have the best time at Princess Celestia's school. Then she closed the door and started to cry.

The young Unicorn put on the cloak she had pieced together and stared at the bag on the floor. She pulled it onto her back, knowing she had no other choice. If she stayed, she'd always be different. The Unicorn with the broken horn. The Unicorn without magic. The Unicorn whose friends left her behind. What kind of life would that be?

She stepped outside, pulled up her hood, and turned back one last time to say good-bye to her cottage. She'd leave tonight, for good. There were other places she could go, and other ponies who might accept her. She couldn't keep pretending she was happy here. This town no longer felt like home.

As she started off into the night, she reminded herself of the worst part. She'd been the brave one that day in the forest. She'd volunteered to go into the cave to get the ball so her friends didn't have to. She'd yelled to Glitter Drops and Spring Rain, telling them there was an ursa minor inside so they wouldn't get hurt. She'd done everything right.

And what did she have to show for it? What did she get for being a good friend?

Nothing, she thought as the lights from the town grew smaller in the distance. *There's nothing left for me there.*